Dedicated to my spirited and inspiring mother.

— Vineeta

Eager Ellis Explores

Illustrated by Vineeta Dhillon
Story by Aananda Verma

Layout and design by Aaron Drown

ISBN 978-1-7353502-0-2

On a bright cool day, a silvery fish named Delilah swam into a shallow bay to lay her eggs.

She scoured the waters to find a safe spot for them.

Soon after she laid her eggs, he got ready to leave. She wanted to get things in order for her babies.

She thought: "I only have a few weeks before the eggs hatch. Then my little babies will need me to look after them."

Delilah turned to take one last look at her eggs. She saw that one egg had rolled away from the rest.

She swam right back and gently whispered: "Now, now, stay with your family until I return, Eager Ellis."

Delilah swished the egg back in place with her top fin and swam away.

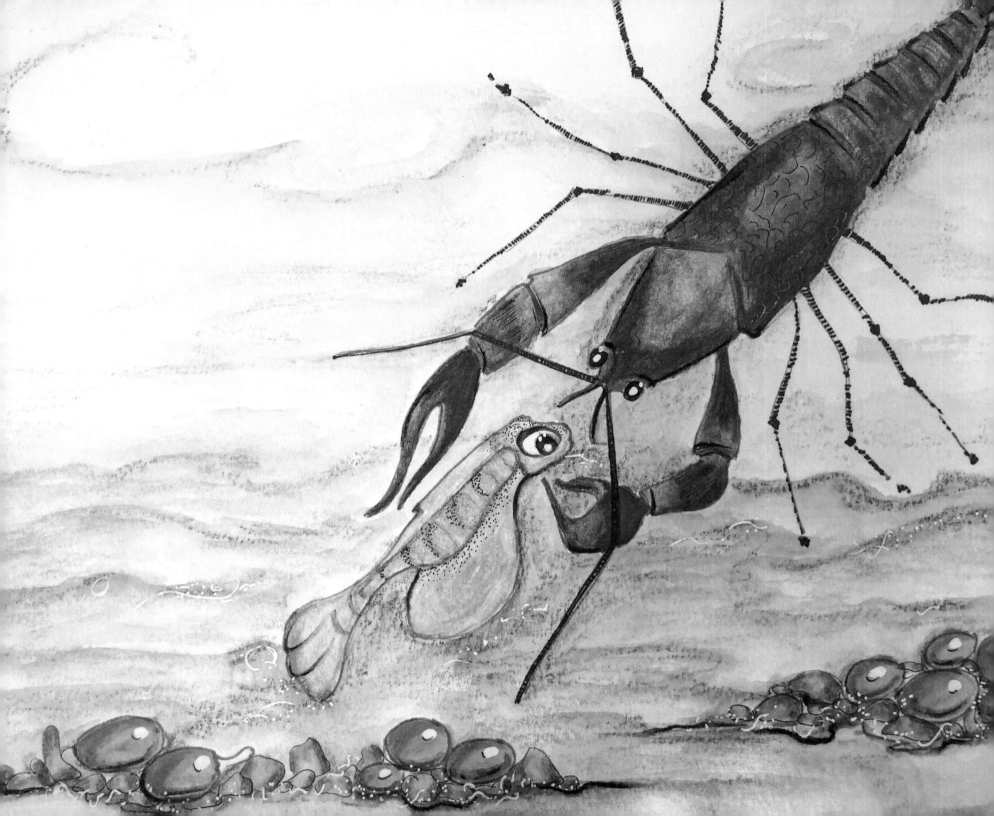

A few weeks later, the same egg wriggled and moved. Eager Ellis hatched before Delilah had returned.

Eager Ellis wanted her mum for cuddles. She felt sad, but was determined to find her. Spirits high, Ellis said to herself: "I am ready to explore the waters to find my mum."

Ellis had barely made it past the first bend in the shallow bay when she came upon a friendly creature who stopped her. Startled, Ellis gasped: "Who are you?"

He said: "Delilah left me in charge of her eggs. My name is Joe, the crawdad. I watched you wriggle out of your shell. Where, may I ask, are you headed?"

"Nice to meet you Joe! I am going in search of my mum," Ellis announced fearlessly. "I have a bit of advice, little Ellis—rest often and do not get too close to large creatures," Joe said.

Ellis thanked him as she headed toward open waters.

**E**llis remembered Joe's advice to rest often.

When she saw a cushiony purple spot, she closed in to take a break. As she reached it, the purple cushion moved to greet her. "Hello! I am Yuri, the urchin."

"Are you my mum," asked Ellis. "I'm afraid not," said Yuri. "Your mama will be just like you—beautiful silvery green with a pink tail, like yours."

"Thank you, Yuri," Ellis said, as she stopped to rest. Later, she swam away to continue her search.

oon, Ellis came upon a shallow cove with beautiful, tall, leafy growth, and bright red fish. Now, these fish were small yet swift as they moved around the stalks. They were playful, and they invited Ellis to join them.

"Catch us if you can," they said.

Amused, Ellis chased them around the cove.

Then she inquired about her mum. "Have you seen a fish just like me, but bigger? She is my mum and I want to find her."

They said that they had not left their playpen and no other creatures had come close. "I'll just have to keep looking" Ellis thought to herself. "Goodbye friends!" Ellis said, as she swam away.

All this swimming made Ellis hungry. She was beginning to wonder "What can I eat? I am hungry!"

As luck would have it, she came upon a spread of multicolored tubes tucked within some greens. The pockets right in front of her were filled with food. Ellis ate until she was full.

Eager Ellis enjoyed her new surroundings as she explored them. Her curiosity drew her to some tall grasses swaying in the water.

She couldn't help but notice some brightly colored corals peeking through the grasses. They looked perfect for nestling.

Ellis decided to rest there for a bit. She dreamed of cuddles with her mum. When she awoke, she noticed a grey shadow beside her.

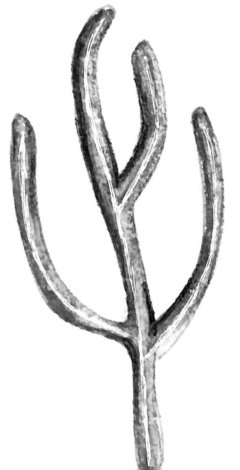

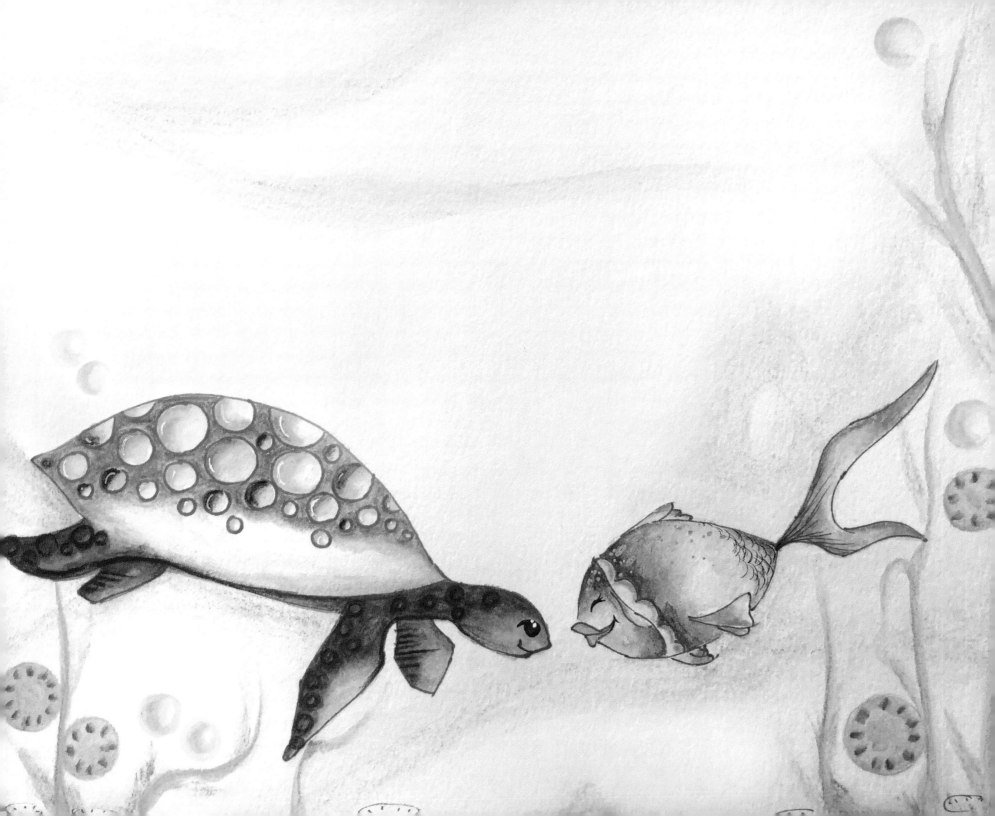

Curious, Ellis swam towards the shadow. She found an adorable creature staring at her. "I am Ellis. You are adorable! Who are you?" she asked.

"Thank you, Ellis. I am Alfie the Turtle," he introduced himself.

"Pleased to meet you, Turtle Alfie," Ellis said. "Can you help me find my mum? She looks like me, much bigger though."

He smiled at Ellis and said: "I have not met your mom. But I will take you to a school of fish who might be able to help you."

They met a school of fish nearby.

A wise old fish helped Ellis understand that mums always come back to their eggs in about twelve weeks. She encouraged Ellis to head back.

"Your mum will come home to you. Please go back. She will be so worried about you if you are not there."

Ellis agreed to go back.

On her way home, Ellis saw a creature like no other. It was so beautiful, with a pearl nesting in the middle.

As Ellis approached, it said: "Hi, I am Juniper the oyster. Are you lost?"

Ellis shook her head, her eyes wide with amazement. "Hi! I am Ellis. No, I am not lost."

Ellis told Juniper all about her search for her mum. She said that she was heading back now.

Juniper was touched by Ellis's tale about her journey. He gave Ellis the pearl to take for her mum.

llis swam back to the shallow bay. Her mum was there!

They rushed toward each other. All Ellis wanted was to cuddle. Both were so happy to see each other.

Then she met her brothers and sisters. She learned all their names. The family promised to stay together forever.

The End.

CPSIA information can be obtained at www.ICGtesting.com
Printed in the USA
BVIW122140211120
593903BV00022B/105